Completely
Clementine

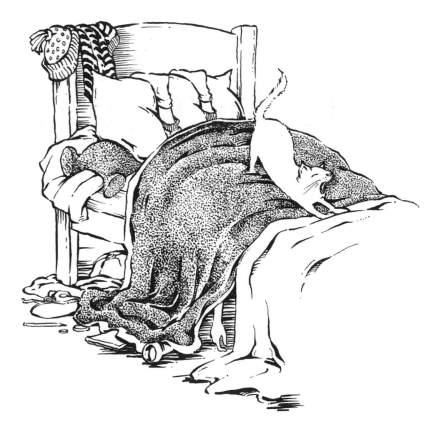

Completely
Clementine

SARA PENNYPACKER

PICTURES BY
Marla Frazee

DISNEY • HYPERION
Los Angeles   New York

Text copyright © 2015 by Sara Pennypacker
Illustrations copyright © 2015 by Marla Frazee

Many thanks to the entire Ramirez family for their help with pages 5, 17, 19, 38, 66, and 169.

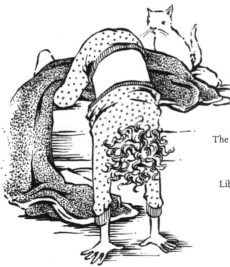

First Hardcover Edition, March 2015
First Paperback Edition, March 2016
10 9 8 7 6 5 4 3 2 1
FAC-025438-15349

This book is set in 15-point Fournier.
Printed in the United States of America

The illustrations for this book were done with pen and ink on Strathmore paper.

Library of Congress Control Number for Hardcover Edition: 2013030583

ISBN 978-1-4231-2438-2

Reinforced binding
Visit www.DisneyBooks.com

SUSTAINABLE FORESTRY INITIATIVE   Certified Sourcing
www.sfiprogram.org
SFI-00993

THIS LABEL APPLIES TO TEXT STOCK

For Ms. Marla,
Clementine's art
and soul
　　—S.P.

To Stephanie Lurie, who
took Clementine's hand
　　—M.F.

Completely
Clementine

As soon as I woke up Monday morning, I flopped onto the floor with my drawing pad. I drew a cow with a sagging-down mouth and rivers of tears flowing from her eyes. When I was finished, that cow looked so sad, my own eyes started to cry a little bit. I wiped them so I could admire what a great job I'd done, and then I smiled.

Because—oh, yes—this drawing was going to crack my father's heart, all right.

I drew about a hundred more teardrops splashing down, and added a couple of ducks paddling around in the puddle of cow-sadness. Then I got dressed and went out into the kitchen, where everyone else was already at the table.

"Okra, would you please pass this to our father?" I asked, sitting down.

My brother, who is obsessed with dinosaurs these days, took the drawing in his teeth and passed it over.

"Hmmm . . ." my dad said. "That is not a bad idea. Not a bad idea at all. A cow with hose-eyes. That could come in handy for . . . well, for putting out fires in a dairy barn, I suppose."

I grabbed the drawing back and stomped into my room to label it "The Crying Cow." Then I crossed out "Crying" and changed it to "Weeping." This is because weeping is a lot sadder than crying; it's tragical, really. I like to use exactly the right word for things.

Then I stomped back and handed it to my brother again. "Collard Greens, please pass this to our father," I growled into my orange juice.

My brother pawed at my drawing and slid it across the table.

This time, my dad didn't even look at it. "Clementine, try to understand," he said. "It was very nice of Mrs. Jacobi to bake that meat loaf for us. She knows how tired your mom is these days, with the baby due so soon. She wanted to help out. It would have been rude not to eat it."

I zipped my mouth into a straight ruler line so it wouldn't say *What about that cow in that meat loaf? Don't you think you were rude to* her*?* Because an important part of not speaking to someone is not speaking to them.

"I'm so mad at my father," I told Margaret as soon as I got on the bus. "Since I turned vegetarian, my mom and Pinto Bean haven't eaten any animals either. But my dad won't do it. He ate meat loaf Saturday night. I'm so mad I can't even talk to him. It's been one day, thirteen hours, and"—I leaned over and checked Margaret's watch—"twenty-one minutes."

"Oh, yeah," Margaret said. "The silent treatment."

"The silent treatment? It's a treatment?"

Margaret nodded hard. "Very effective. Hold out for a lot."

"What do you mean?"

"The last time I used the silent treatment was in the spring, when my mother told me what kind of wedding she wasn't having. I'm *still* getting stuff out of that one."

A couple of years ago, Margaret had watched a real prince and princess get married on television. Since then, she'd considered herself an expert on royal weddings. So when she learned her mother was getting remarried, she figured she'd get to run the wedding. "I wasn't there for her first one, to my father," she'd told me, "but I can make up for that now. This one with Alan is going to be a doozy."

She got a little carried away, planning this and planning that. One problem: she forgot to tell her mother about any of it.

When Margaret's mother finally heard about the special wave from the balcony, the satin train with fourteen footmen to carry it, the carriage ride, and the hundred other details, she said, "NO."

"What part NO?" Margaret had asked.

Margaret's mother had meant NO to all of it, which made Margaret go berserk. "Three whole days I didn't talk to her," Margaret said. "On the last day, I even added my invisible treatment."

"What's that?"

"You act as if the person is invisible to you. I looked right through her, as if she weren't there. You should use it with your father."

"I don't think I could do that," I told her after I'd tried to imagine it for a while. "My father's the opposite of invisible."

"Too bad—it's very powerful. It made my mother give in. She agreed to have a flower girl— me—and to get me a new dress, whatever I want. And tomorrow, I'm getting the best part: new shoes."

This was so ridiculous I snort-laughed. "Shoes?

Margaret, getting new shoes isn't winning any-thing." I thought back to when I had to get new sneakers last fall. "In fact, I think shopping for shoes is a punishment."

"Oh, these shoes are winning something, all right. These shoes are going to be *high heels*."

I felt my jaw fall down. It took all my power to crank it back up to my chin by the time we pulled in to school.

First thing when I walked into Room 3B, my teacher asked, "Yet?" and I answered, "Not yet."

We have been "Yet?"ing and "Not yet"ing each other about waiting for babies since spring. First it was me "Yet?"ing him, but after his baby was finally born in May, he started "Yet?"ing me and I started "Not yet"ing him back.

"And Not yet about a name, either," I answered to his next question as I took my seat.

When the Pledge was over, Mr. D'Matz called us for Circle Sharing Time. "As you know, this is the last week of school, and we have a lot to accomp—"

Mr. D'Matz waited while all the kids cheered about school being over. All the kids except me, that is. I'm happy about no school for the whole summer too, of course—I've got a lot of great stuff planned. What I'm not happy about is the rest of it. The Starting-Over-with-a-New-Class-in-the-Fall part, and the What-If-I-Don't-Get-a-Nice-Teacher part. And most of all, the Saying-Good-bye-to-Mr.-D'Matz part.

I do not like saying good-bye.

"Thursday is the last day of school," Mr. D'Matz started up again, "so we've only got four days. We'll have to hurry to get our work finished, because I know we'll want to leave plenty of time to say good-bye."

* * *

At recess, Rasheed and Maria ran up to me. "What
did Margaret say?" they asked.

Maria and Rasheed have been asking me this every day since they fell in love this spring. Actually, it was Rasheed who fell in love, and Maria just said *I don't care, sure, whatever,* about being in love back. When they heard that Margaret was an expert in royal weddings, they started passing along questions about how to get married.

"Margaret said you should have about a thousand lights, but you shouldn't see the wires," I told them. "When Princess Diana got married, they used ferrets to run the wires through pipes under the ground."

Rasheed sighed. "I don't know anybody with a ferret. And my cat's too fat to go through underground pipes."

"No problem," said Maria. "Flo-Max will do it. Lizards like to go into skinny places. Once he got loose and a week later he crawled out of the bathtub drain. But ask Margaret about those arm-gloves she said I had to wear. Do I need them if it's summertime, or are they just for winter?"

When they ran off, I took a marker from my pocket and added a new exclamation point to the arm reminder I've been keeping since all this started: NO WEDDINGS FOR ME!!!!!!!!

Tuesday morning I had to put my newest sad-animal drawing beside my dad's coffee cup, because he was already off at work. "Petrified Piglets" was my best one yet: baby pigs running away from a farmer holding a hot dog roll and a jar of spicy mustard.

"I wish you could hurry up and have our baby," I told my mom as I slid into my seat. "I wish you could have it before Thursday, so I could let my teacher know what a *good* baby is like."

My mom handed me an English muffin and a jar of almond butter. "You mean his new little boy isn't a good baby?" she asked.

I shook my head as I spread the almond butter into a perfect circle. "He sounds like a dud," I answered. "Mr. D'Matz is always telling us things like 'Wow, yesterday he drank an extra ounce of milk!' and 'He really loves to look at his mobile!' as if those were the most exciting tricks any human in the world ever performed. I think it's just that he doesn't know any better—this is the only baby he's got. So I wish I could tell him about ours."

My mom patted her belly. "You think our baby's going to be more interesting than his, is that it?"

I nodded. "And more fun."

"Well, it might not be all fun," my mom said. "At least not in the beginning." She went into her bedroom and came out a minute later with a folded-up piece of paper. "Do you remember this? It's a letter to your brother when he was a week old. You dictated it to me and we went to the post office so you could mail it to him."

I took the note and read it:

Dear Spinach,
I love you. I would love you more if you stopped crying. Also, if you did something. Besides crying.
Love,
Your sister, Clementine

"Oh, right," I said. "I do remember. Yam was kind of a dud too. Still, could you try to have the baby early? There are only a few more days of school left, and it would be great to brag about it—I mean *share* about it—at Circle Sharing Time. So how about you try to have it on . . ." I got up to check the calendar. "Auurrgghh! Not today! Try really hard not to let the baby be born today!"

"Why not? What's today?"

I couldn't believe she had forgotten something this important. "Mom! Today is the second anniversary of when I threw up on the subway! This would be a terrible day for the baby to be born!"

My mother laughed. "Well, it would also be a terrible day because we're not ready here." A panicky look came over her face then. "We're not ready yet. We're not ready yet!" she cried. She grabbed the edge of the table and squeezed until her knuckles went white, then she took a couple of deep breaths. "It's okay, it's okay," she said in a Calm-Down-Now voice. "July second is still two weeks away."

July second is our baby's due date. This is not

like a library due date, because we're not just borrowing our baby. And it's not like a sell-by date on groceries, because our baby isn't going to start to get moldy and rot after that. What it is, is the date our baby's aiming to be born. My mother doesn't keep a calendar inside her belly, but somehow, our baby is going to know that around July second we're going to be expecting to see it.

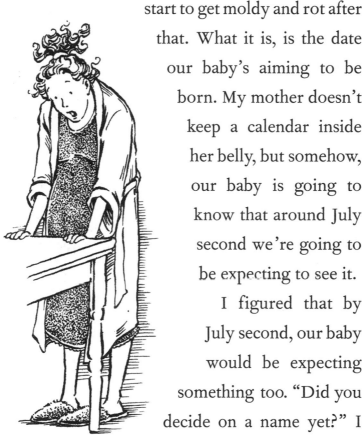

I figured that by July second, our baby would be expecting something too. "Did you decide on a name yet?" I asked as I put my backpack

on. "Because I've got some new thing-names for you. . . ."

When I first heard about a new baby coming, I wanted it to have a food name. My name is a fruit, which I used to hate but now I like. I call my brother vegetable names to make it fair, which he used to hate but now he likes too. So I thought our new brother or sister should have a food name too, so he or she wouldn't feel left out.

My dad said yes, because he'd always wanted a kid named Noodle. "It's so good," he pleaded, "for either a boy or a girl!" But my mother said *Absolutely not!*

Then I tried a compromise, which means nobody wins, but nobody loses, either. "How about a thing-name then? Let's give the baby a name that's also a thing, at least."

My father loved this idea too. My mother rolled

her eyes at all his suggestions: Lug Nut, Pencil, Q-tip, and Noodle again. But she didn't hate the thing-name idea. "Dawn," she said. "That's a lovely name. Or maybe Colt, if it's a boy."

"So, do you want to hear them?" I asked.

"Maybe later. We still have two weeks. I have a feeling the perfect name will show up by then." She patted my backpack and turned me toward the door. "Right now, it's time for school."

At recess, I gave Maria the bad news about the gloves: Yes, summer or winter. "But Margaret says if it's a summer wedding, you could skip the fur cape. She also says you should start practicing the royal wave."

"The royal wave?"

I put my hand up beside my face to demonstrate what Margaret had taught me. "Just a swivel of the hand, nothing flappy. And always above the shoulder and below the crown."

While Maria was practicing the special wave, Rasheed came over, dragging Joe. "Joe's going to be my best man," he said. "But he says he'll only do it if his dog Buddy can be in the wedding too. Ask Margaret if that's okay."

"Tell Margaret that for a dog, he barely slobbers at all," Joe added.

And right then, I saw something I'd never seen before. Something really amazing.

"Joe!" I yelled. "I see your knees!"

Joe ignored me and went on telling about some great tricks his dog could do to entertain the wedding guests.

I grabbed him by the shoulders and looked straight into his face. "Joe," I said again, "you don't understand. *I. SEE. YOUR. KNEES!!!*"

And then his eyes got so big I thought they were

going to pop out of his head. "You mean . . ."

Very slowly, as if he was afraid he wasn't going to see what he was really, really, hoping he was going to see, he looked down at his legs. When his eyes saw his knees peeking out from under

his shorts, his mouth fell open. He hugged me, then he hugged Maria and Rasheed. Then he apologized for hugging us. Then he took off around the playground high-fiving everybody else. When he ran out of kids to high-five, he leaped up  and punched the air. "Yes!" he screamed when he got back to us. "It's started! My growth spurt has started!"

Joe has been the shortest kid in our class since kindergarten. He's been praying all year for a sudden growth spurt, and now he looked happier than I'd ever seen him. "If you keep this up, you'll have to bend over to hand Rasheed the ring at the wedding," I said.

Joe smiled bigger still, and I think even his teeth had gotten taller.

"They might have to raise the fourth-grade doorways by the time school starts in September," I said.

Joe's grin nearly split his cheeks off. "I should probably warn Principal Rice, just to be fair."

"You should," I agreed. "Your growth spurt is astoundishing."

Joe's smile collapsed. He narrowed his eyes. "What do you mean, astoundishing? That's not a word."

"Of course it is. I use it all the time."

"I know you do. But it's still not a word."

"Oh, yeah? How come you never told me before?"

Joe shrugged. "I guess I wasn't tall enough before," he said.

As soon as I got inside, I asked my teacher if I could use his grown-up dictionary, the one with all the words in the world, while the other kids began cleaning out their desks.

"It's not here!" I cried, after I'd searched and searched. "I found *astounding* and *astonishing*, but not *astoundishing*. It's missing."

And then my teacher said something I did N-O-T, *not* want to hear. "That's because it's not a real word."

I closed that dictionary so hard I probably

flattened a bunch of words. "But it has to be! It's a great word."

Mr. D'Matz put his coffee cup down. "Well, let's think about this interesting question: What is the job of language?"

When my teacher says, "Well, let's think about this interesting question," it means he's too lazy to figure out a lesson and he wants a kid to do it for him. Usually I try to help him out, but just then I was too upset, so I folded my arms and waited for him to answer it himself. Which he did.

"Language's job is to communicate as clearly as possible. On the one hand, we have rules—like grammar, and spelling, and a set of words we agree to use—so everybody can understand each other easily. But on the other hand, language has to grow and change, too. People make up new words to describe new things. So maybe you've made up a new word. You shouldn't use it in a school paper, and you'd get it marked wrong on a spelling test. But you can use it with me, all right? Because I agree that it's a great word."

Mr. D'Matz put the dictionary back in its place. "And speaking of things that grow and change . . ."

I clapped my hands over my ears, fast, because I knew what was coming. All last week, he had tried to tell me about what a great year I'd had, and how I was ready to say good-bye to him and head off for fourth grade. He'd been getting trickier about sneaking up on me about this, but I was getting trickier about avoiding it. "I just remembered I might have left a bologna sandwich in my desk in September," I said. "So I'd better go clean it out now."

3

On the bus ride home, Margaret asked me how the silent treatment was going.

"I didn't say a single word all night," I said. I checked her watch. "So now it's been two days, twenty hours, and fifty-six minutes. It's really hard, though, Margaret."

"Is it harder than not scratching when you had poison ivy last summer? Is not talking to him harder than that?"

"That doesn't count," I decided, after I'd thought about it for a minute. "When I had poison ivy, my mother taped socks over my hands. That made it easier."

Margaret sat back, thinking. "Well, I *guess* you could tape socks over your lips," she said after a while. "But clean, never-been-used ones, of course. I could get some for you."

I said *Thanks but no thanks* to that, and changed the subject. "Maria and Rasheed want to know if Joe's dog can be in the wedding."

"A dog in the wedding? In the actual wedding? Of course not!" Margaret sputtered. "But find out if Buddy could pull the carriage. Otherwise, they're going to have to get a horse."

When I got home, I found my mother on the kitchen floor.

"Mom!" I cried. "What are you doing?" Although I could see: she was scrubbing the underneath of the stove . . . with a toothbrush!

"Getting ready," she answered, in a voice that sounded as puffy and sweaty as she looked. "There's a baby's coming soon, you know."

"But, um, it's not going to live in the oven," I said. "We have a crib, remember? So . . . ?"

Just then my dad poked his head into the kitchen and signaled for me to come back into the living room with him. I did, but I pressed my mouth closed hard so no words could slip out.

"Your mother," he said in an extra-loud voice, "is *completely sane.*" At the same time, he was pooching out his belly and making crazy-circles at his temples with his fingers. He was telling me that Mom was acting a little nuts because of being pregnant.

Which had been happening more and more lately. On Saturday, she washed and folded all the baby's clothes, which she had already washed and folded on Friday. On Sunday, she color-coded everything in our hall closet. And last night after dinner, she alphabetized the food in our refrigerator. Dad says what she's doing is called *nesting*, and it's a perfectly normal stage that happens right before a baby is born.

It didn't seem that normal to me, though. Actually, it made me a little worried.

My dad left to go to work. And suddenly, more than anything, I wished I could call him back so he could tell me again that everything was fine with my mom.

I needed to break his heart with my sad-animal drawings pretty soon, because I didn't know how much longer I could keep up the silent treatment.

So I went into my room to make an extra-sad one—one that would *work*. I decided on a turkey looking at a November calendar with drops of worry-sweat fountaining out of its forehead. I labeled it "THANKSGIVING TRAGEDY" and turned the two "T"s into hatchets, to help my dad get the point. Then I tucked the drawing into my pocket and went to find him.

He was in the lobby, hanging a big yellow sun from the chandelier. I opened my mouth to ask why, but just in time I remembered, and I clamped it shut. Dad must have noticed my *How come?* eyes, because he said, "Sunday is the Summer Solstice. It's a pretty important day—the first day of summer."

I watched him tack up a WELCOME SUMMER! sign, and then I remembered why I had come up here in the first place. I pulled out my drawing and handed it to him.

And my wish came true! His whole face crashed

down in sadness—his eyes, his mouth, his ears, and even his beard.

"Clementine," he said with a big sigh, "could you please try to remember what we talked about after *Beauty and the Beast*?" Then he turned away and pressed the elevator UP button. As he got in, his shoulders sagged down as if they were sad too.

I would have been really happy that my drawing had done such a good job, except that now I was

too busy trying *not* to think about the *Beauty and the Beast* time.

Because remembering that would have wrecked everything.

Wednesday morning, after "Yet?"ing and "Not yet"ing, I told Mr. D'Matz the great idea I'd had.

"You think I'd make a good fourth-grade teacher?" he repeated. "Well, thank you. That's a compliment."

I nodded. "So you should switch. In September."

"That's not how it works," he said. "There are two fourth-grade teachers in this school already, and they're both planning on coming back. Besides, I really like it here in third grade."

"Oh, sure, you like *us* in third grade," I explained, "because we're such a great class. You never know what's coming next year. I've seen the second graders eating lunch and, let me tell you, some of them are . . ." Luckily, just then I remembered some words my grandmother had used to describe my father when he was little. "*Hellions!* Some of them might even be *feral*. They might bite you, and you'd have to check them for rabies, and—"

My teacher laughed as if I had told him a good joke. "Well, they won't be you guys, that's for sure. You're a special class, all right. But I like teaching this age group. I like seeing how much third graders change during the year. Take you, for example, Clementine."

"No thanks," I said. "Let's *not* take me for example. Let's take Joe instead. He's really changed lately. Hey, Joe, come on up here and show Mr. D'Matz how tall you've gotten!"

And it worked. Joe's growth spurt tricked our teacher into forgetting about saying *Good-bye, Clementine, you've really changed, so you're ready for fourth grade.*

He didn't stay tricked for long, though. In math, we did a short review and then, as he collected our Fraction Blaster packets, he started in again. "It's added up to quite a year," he said, and suddenly I knew we weren't talking about quarters and thirds anymore.

"I'm so proud of each and every one of you, of how much you've learned and grown. You've mastered a lot of material, and now you're ready for new challenges. I'm reminded of the mother bird and her baby birds . . ."

Before he could get going with his favorite story

about how great it is when perfectly happy, unsuspecting little birds get kicked off their branches, I shot my hand up.

"Yes, Clementine?"

"I have to go to the principal's office," I said.

"Right now? Is it an emergency?"

"Yes," I said, glad he'd thought up this good reason. "An emergency I forgot about because it just happened."

Mr. D'Matz looked confused by that, so I jumped up and left. I stomped down the hall to the principal's office, which is something I have done so many times this year, I am surprised the hall doesn't have a path worn into it. When Mrs. Rice answered my knock, I stomped in, sat down, crossed my arms over my chest, and aimed my sting-ray eyes at her. This is called Sending a Message.

"Hello, Clementine," she said, completely ignoring my message. "I haven't seen you in a while. What's on your mind?"

"I think you should promote him," I said. "Our teacher. He's really grown this year. He's really mastered the material and is ready for a new challenge. So I think you should kick him off the branch—I mean, promote him to fourth grade. You're the principal, you can do it."

"Well, but moving to a higher grade isn't a promotion for a teacher. All of our grades provide teachers the same amount of . . . um . . ." Mrs. Rice

rubbed her chin and looked up at the ceiling, as if she hoped a good word might be hanging there. "Well, never mind," she said after a minute of not finding it. "But speaking of growing, I'd hardly recognize you from the beginning of the year, you've grown so much, Clementine."

I jumped off the chair and looked down at my legs to see if a growth spurt had snuck up on me, too.

Mrs. Rice chuckled. "No, I didn't mean you're taller, although I expect you are. I should have said, you've really matured this year. Why, I haven't seen you in here for a chat about your behavior since . . ." She stopped to think.

"Three Wednesdays ago," I sighed. "My feet were too bored to stay under my desk during a film the nurse showed us about nutrition."

Mrs. Rice's head snapped up. "Not the Super-power Vitamins film? Where the apples wear little capes? The one with the sword-fighting carrots?"

I nodded. My feet were getting itchy again just thinking about how boring that film was.

"Good grief, I know that one. Just between us, Clementine, my feet would have gotten bored too, if I had to sit through that film. So that trip to my office doesn't count. And before that, the last time you were here was . . . well, I can't even remember.

Which is quite a difference—in the beginning of the year, you were a regular visitor. You've gotten so much better about controlling your impulses, and thinking ahead about consequences. So you see, I think you're the one who's ready for the promotion."

Suddenly, I was all finished being there, so I got up to leave.

"Have a wonderful summer, Clementine," said Mrs. Rice. "I'll see you next year."

I stopped in the doorway. And mind-reading must be something they teach at principal school.

"Yes, Clementine," Principal Rice promised to the question I hadn't asked out loud. "I will be right here."

When we got off the bus, Margaret led me up to her apartment to show me her new shoes. She took me right into her closet, without even asking if I'd had a shower that day, the way she usually does, and slid a pink box off the top shelf.

"Wow," I said when she lifted the lid. "Are they real gold?"

"Of course. Probably. Maybe. Don't breathe so hard on them," Margaret said. "You'll fog up the patina."

So I turned my head and did side-breathing

while I admired Margaret's sparkly new shoes for a while. "How tall are they?" I asked when I thought we had done enough admiring.

"Oh, eight or nine inches. Maybe ten."

"I don't think so, Margaret," I said. Then I held one of the shoes against my left forearm and measured it. "The heel is two inches high," I told Margaret.

"How do you know that?" she asked.

"Because it fits between Betelgeuse and Alula Borealis, which are exactly two inches apart." I held the shoe up against my arm again to show her. "Well, plus my fingernail. Two inches and a fingernail. Are they hard to walk in?"

"Hold on, hold on," Margaret said. "You've *named* your *freckles?*"

"Actually, my dad did," I said. "He named them after stars. We played a game about the constellations on my arms. Orion's over here and—"

Suddenly, thinking about my dad made my eyes sting and my throat hurt. "Never mind," I said. "Those heels are two inches tall, Margaret. Not ten."

"And a fingernail."

"And a fingernail. Which is pretty high, all right," I admitted. "I can't believe your mother let you get them."

"She didn't want to," Margaret said. "She's afraid I'll break my neck. That's how effective my silent treatment is. How's yours going?"

"I'm still doing it," I said. I checked her watch. "Three days, twenty-one hours, and forty-nine minutes now. But it's so hard. In fact, I think it's the hardest thing I've ever done."

Margaret's eyebrows shot up. "Really? It's harder than . . ."

Margaret looked at me and I looked at her. I knew we were both thinking about the same thing, the thing that was so bad neither one of us wanted to say it out loud: when my kitten Moisturizer went missing last winter.

"I don't know if it's harder than that," I said, after I'd thought about it for a while. "But it's definitely lonelier. It makes me miss my dad. It feels like he's in another country, far away, and I can't go there with him."

Margaret's face crumpled a little at that, and I remembered: Margaret's mother was going on a honeymoon with Alan after the wedding. To Paris, France, which really is in another country, far away.

"Are you going to miss your mother next week?" I asked.

Margaret put her shoes back on the shelf, then she went back into her room.

I followed her. "Are you?"

She nodded. "It's the first time she's ever left."

"Do you wish you could go with them?" I asked.

Margaret made the horror face she always makes when her mother and Alan are kissing. "Are you crazy? Do you know what a honeymoon *is*?"

I nodded yes, then shook my head no. "Tell me."

Margaret shuddered and jumped back, as if some newlyweds were about to burst in and start honeymooning right in front of her. "You're lucky you don't know," she muttered. "You should keep it that way."

After she shuddered a few more times, she said, "Besides, I *want* to stay here. My father's coming from California, and Mitchell and I are going to spend the whole week in a fancy hotel with him while our mother and Alan are gone. Room service and cleaning ladies every day."

Margaret reached down to give her cat a pat. "Even Mascara is coming. We're going there right after the wedding." Mascara scrambled under the

bed, so I didn't think he was too interested in the idea of living in a hotel for a whole week.

But I was. When I was little, I read a book about a girl named Eloise, who lived in a hotel her whole life. "Elevators and vending machines and spying on famous people for a whole week?"

"And sanitized toilets, and fresh, sterilized bathrobes, and individual wrapped-up bars of soap every day. And *cleaning ladies*, Clementine. The best part is, my father says I can stay in the room while they're cleaning it, so I can pick up some professional tips. Hey, I know—you should come visit!"

I wasn't sure about that. I did want to go to an Eloise kind of hotel, of course, but sometimes being in a room that's too neat makes me feel itchy. So instead of deciding, I said, "Hey, Alan's ashtray is almost finished. Want to see it?" to throw her off that idea.

When Margaret learned that Alan was going to move in with them after the wedding, she went all historical. It wasn't the idea of Alan living there, it was his pipe. How would she know where the pipe germs were? was the big worry. But then she had the good idea of giving him an ashtray for his pipe to live in, and the second good idea of having me make it. Margaret got me one of Alan's backup pipes, so I could make sure it would fit; my mom gave me a big slab of clay from her friend Astrid, who is a potter; and my dad had helped me with the design.

Margaret did want to see it, of course, because she knew this wasn't just any old regular ashtray.

"I'm only going to look, though," she said. "I don't touch stuff like that."

We rode the elevator down to the workshop, and I swept the dishtowel off the ashtray with a big *ta-da!* "Look," I said, "here's the bedroom,

where the pipe rests when Alan's not smoking it. Here's the dining room—that's where Alan can fill it up. And over here, a swimming pool—that's where you can make him wash it."

"So when are you going to bake it clean?" Margaret asked. "The wedding's on Saturday, you know."

No matter how many times I tell her that you fire pottery in a kiln to harden the clay, she still insists that it's a germ-destroying strategy. I have given up trying to get Margaret to understand art.

"We fired the ashtray at my mom's friend's studio last weekend. That's why it's hard," I explained. "Tonight we're going to glaze it, then it gets fired in the kiln again, hotter this time. Don't worry—it'll be ready in time."

And I suddenly remembered something. When my father heard the date that Margaret's mother and Alan were getting married, he said it was an extremely lucky one. It was the same date he and my mom had gotten married, except thirteen years later. So that meant Saturday was also my parents' anniversary.

All the wedding stuff reminded me to ask Maria and Rasheed's newest question. "Joe said his dog Buddy could pull the carriage along the parade route, no problem. But Maria's worried about what he'll do when they release the hundred white doves. She's afraid he'll chase them. What do you think?"

Margaret shook her head as if this was the most ridiculous thing she'd ever heard. "The carriage ride is *before* the ceremony; the doves are released *after*. But just to be sure, have them take Buddy to the park to practice not chasing the pigeons."

I wrote this down on my arm, being careful not to cover any freckle-stars, so I'd remember it tomorrow. Then I went back to my own apartment to start a new drawing.

Let me tell you, it is not easy to make a clam look terrified. The problem is the shell—it's very hard to put any expression at all on someone whose face is in a seashell—but I did it. I took the drawing into my dad's room and propped it up on his pillow. Just before I left, I noticed the book he keeps on his bed-side table—the one I helped him start a while ago. It's called *The Building Manager*, and in it,

we keep track of the interesting things that happen in our building.

I opened it up to see if he'd written anything new. He had. THE BUILDING MANAGER'S DAUGHTER HAD STOPPED SPEAKING TO HIM, I read. THIS MADE THE BUILDING MANAGER TERRIBLY, TERRIBLY SAD.

I quick-flipped back through the pages. Mostly the stories were fun to remember. I read about the time the ice cream truck blew a tire in front of our building, and we bought all the ice cream from the driver and threw a neighborhood party on the rooftop before it melted. I read about the night the power went out and everyone came down to the lobby with candles and we told ghost stories.

Then I got to one that wasn't so good—the time I sold everybody's charity giveaways to each other. The problem about that was: the things my neighbors were giving away had been presents from other neighbors. When people found out their presents had been tossed, they were mad at each other for a long time. At the end of that chapter, I'd written in the book that the building manager's daughter promised she'd think ahead about doing things before she did them, so she wouldn't get into trouble.

I stared down at that promise. Since then, I usually had tried to think ahead. But sometimes—okay, fine: lots of times—I still didn't.

I closed the book and shoved it back onto the table. As I did, some papers fell out. I picked them up. My sad-animal drawings.

My father was saving them all.

6

Like the fruit that is my name, sometimes I feel divided into sections. Thursday morning, the last day of school, some of my Clementine sections were worrying about how hard it would be to say *Good-bye, I sure grew a lot and now I'm ready for the challenges of fourth grade!* to Mr. D'Matz.

I had stayed awake late the night before, remembering my promise to think about things before I did them. And remembering something else: when my grandparents moved to Florida, everyone said good-bye except me—it had been too hard.

But afterward I felt even worse from *not* saying good-bye to them. I finally had to write a letter saying *Good-bye, I'm sorry I didn't say good-bye,* so I could stop crying.

So now some of my sections were thinking ahead, and worrying about how bad I might feel all summer if I *didn't* say good-bye to my teacher today.

I sat by myself at the back of the bus so my two parts could argue it out on the way to school. Finally, just when the bus pulled into the parking circle, I knew: I *was* going to let my teacher say good-bye to me, and I *was* going to say it back.

But when I got into our classroom for the last first time of a third-grade day, I had a terrible surprise. Our substitute, Mrs. Nagle, was draping her jacket over the back of Mr. D'Matz's chair.

"How come you're here? Where's our teacher?"

"He's absent today," she said.

"All day?" I gasped.

"All day, I'm afraid."

"But he wouldn't do that. We didn't say good-bye, and today's our last chance!" I pressed my hands hard to my eyes to let them know I did N-O-T, *not* want them to cry about this.

Mrs. Nagle scooted back in her chair so she could study me better. "I'm sorry," she said, and I could tell she really meant it, as if maybe she had forgotten to say good-bye to somebody once, and then it had been too late. "I know he didn't plan to be away today. He had a last-minute conflict. These things happen."

She held out a tissue. As I reached for it, Mrs. Nagle looked down at the words over my wrist— *BRING BUDDY TO PARK—NO CHASING PIGEONS!* I could see her remembering that she had learned about arm reminders from me last time she was here.

"You're Clementine, right?" she said with a
little smile. Then she invited me to stay up at her
desk while the other kids were still coming in.
"You can help me get organized here."

I stayed up at Mrs. Nagle's desk even though
she didn't really need any help getting organized,
and even though I was still pretty upset about my
teacher being absent. Because *I* had remembered
something about *her*, too.

Last time she was here, she'd brought a picture of her new baby nephew, and although he was wrapped up in a blanket, I could tell he was half rat. Since this is the kind of thing you usually only get to read about in a supermarket checkout line, I'd been thinking about this kid a lot.

"How's your nephew?" I asked politely. "Is he squeaking yet?"

"Is he speaking yet?" she asked. "No, he's still just a baby—"

"How about cheese?" I asked. "Do you notice that he likes cheese a lot? And do you have any new pictures in there?" I asked. "One that maybe shows him running around?"

Mrs. Nagle looked at me as though she had no idea what I was talking about and began digging around in her bag. All she took out was a plan book and a pen.

"Where's your stuff?" I asked. "Where's your mug and your tissue box and your stickers?"

"You have a good memory," Mrs. Nagle said. "I did bring all those things last time. But I packed lightly this time. I'm only here for . . ." She looked at her watch. "Six hours and twenty minutes. Not long at all. Today we'll just be . . ." She pulled out a note from her plan book and read it aloud. From the neat handwriting, I could tell it was from our teacher. "'Reporting about our year, packing the last things up, saying our good-byes, and handing out report cards.'"

Right after the Pledge, she got started on the "reporting about our year" thing. "Mr. D'Matz has asked each of you to share with the class the best thing you learned in third grade. Who would like to go first?"

Charlie raised his hand. "The best thing I

learned this year was how to get a vending machine to give out extra candy bars."

Mrs. Nagle's head shot up at that. "Really? Your teacher taught you that?"

Charlie looked confused. "No. Baxter taught us that."

Baxter had only been in our school for four days in September, but four days with Baxter was plenty, let me tell you. He was a one-kid gang of criminals, and when he left, we all figured it was to go to prison.

Willy went next. "Baxter taught me how to pick a lock with a hairpin," he said. "Without leaving finger-prints. Want to see?"

We all did, of course, but Mrs. Nagle stood and clapped her hands. "From now on we're going to hear about school things," she said. "The best lesson, the best project, the best book—that kind of thing."

Half the kids' heads clunked to their desks, including mine.

"Who'd like to share one of those things?" Mrs. Nagle asked.

Nobody raised a hand.

"Never mind," she said with a sigh. "Let's move on to the packing and saying good-bye."

We got out the boxes we'd brought in and started filling them up. I packed my cardboard Sphinx, my "Welcome to the Future" rocket hat, and my *Charlotte's Web* barn diorama. With each thing that disappeared into the boxes, our classroom looked a little lonelier.

While we packed up, we visited each other and said good-bye. And I learned something: it wasn't saying good-bye I hated, it was not knowing if I'd see the person again.

For instance, I couldn't say good-bye to our hamsters Zippy and Bump, because they were going home with Mr. D'Matz and I didn't know if they'd ever be back at school. "Have a good summer," I told them. "Hope that dud baby isn't too boring for you." But I didn't actually say good-bye.

But to the rest of the kids, I did. And it was fine! "Good-bye, see you next year," I said to all the kids in my class. Well, all the kids except Olive, who likes you to talk Olive-talk to her. "Golivood-bolivye, solivee yolivou nolivext yolivear," I said to her. And that was fine too.

But every time I said a good-bye, it reminded me of the one I hadn't said. The hardest one. The one to Mr. D'Matz.

At recess, I told Rasheed and Maria the idea of making Buddy practice with pigeons.

"That's good," Maria said. "Because if Buddy chomped up a bunch of doves, it would probably ruin that fairy-tale effect thing Margaret's always talking about."

"Did you watch *Danger Rangers* last week, Clementine?" Rasheed asked.

"What? Yes. Now, Margaret also said to remind you about the bells. The hundred doves are supposed to fly out of a bell place when they start ringing. She said Maria has to pick out a good bell song."

Rasheed was looking at me with melty eyes and a goofy smile. "Make it a song you like, Clementine," he said. "Because now I love you."

Maria and I both glared at him. "Me?" I said. "You can't love me. You love Maria."

"I used to," Rasheed agreed. "But Maria's

mother doesn't allow television, and you get to watch *Danger Rangers*, so now I love you."

"Rasheed, being in love isn't like breakfast cereal! It's not like one day you love oatmeal and the next day you change your mind and it's Frosty Pops and hold the bananas. Tell him, Maria!"

Maria was squint-eyeing me. "Am I the oatmeal or the Frosty Pops?" she asked.

"What?"

"In that thing you said. Am I the oatmeal, or the Frosty Pops?"

"I . . . well, you're the first thing, I guess. The oatmeal. But the point is, he can't just stop loving you and boom! start lov—"

"I don't want to be the oatmeal. I'll be the Frosty Pops. You be the oatmeal."

"I don't want to be the oatmeal *or* the Frosty Pops!" I yelled. "I don't want to be any cereal at all!"

"Well, I'm not going to be in love anymore, if it means I'm just a glump of oatmeal." Maria raised her hand and swivel-waved it. "Remember," she said to me, "above the shoulder, below the crown." Then she skipped off.

I turned to Rasheed. "You can't love me," I told

84

him. "I don't allow it."

"Too late," said Rasheed. "It's already happened. I know because I feel glozzled when I look at you."

"*Glozzled? Glozzled* isn't even a word."

"Yes it is. It's exactly the word for how you feel when you're in love, and I feel it when I look at you."

"Well, just feel glozzled by yourself, okay?" I said. "Because I definitely don't feel glozzled back."

After school, Margaret came to my apartment, because her mother was working late at the bank and Mitchell had a baseball game.

We made a tall stack of toast and brought it

to the kitchen table. Margaret waited until my mother sat down, then she chose the chair opposite her. Ever since Margaret learned my mother was pregnant, she has been keeping a safe distance away, as if she suspects our baby is a bomb just waiting to explode all over her. I used to think she was being ridiculous, but I've seen my mother's belly up close now, and I'm kind of keeping my distance too.

"So," my mom said, "Clementine says you have big plans for the summer, Margaret."

Margaret beamed. "I've worked out a brand-new cleaning schedule for my bedroom: Mondays—reorganize my closet; Wednesdays—wash and fold all my clothes; Fridays—vacuum and polish. It's going to be a great summer."

"Not that, Margaret!" I cried. "The good thing!"

Margaret looked confused.

"California? The *commercial?*"

"Oh, right," she said. "My dad's filming a commercial for a water park in August. I'm going to be in it. I can be either one of the lucky kids who gets to go there, or one of the sad ones who doesn't, whichever I want. But about my summer cleaning schedule. I forgot to say the best part: Every other Saturday, we're going to steam-clean my rug!"

Margaret's face melted into the magical dream of this extra-clean summer. My mother and I raised our eyebrows at each other in secret You-Must-Be-Kidding faces.

"Well," my mom said at last, "I bet you're excited about the wedding."

This crashed Margaret right out of her magical dream. She scowled and shot *me* the

secret You-Must-Be-Kidding face.

I explained to my mom about Margaret being an expert on royal weddings. "If this country ever goes back to having a king and a queen," I added, "and they have princes and princesses who need to get married, Margaret's going to be the one they call."

"Maybe you'll grow up to be a wedding planner," my mother said to Margaret. "That's someone who organizes everything about weddings."

Margaret dropped her toast, and she didn't even jump up to get the DustBuster. "That's a *job*?" She gasped. "And people would *pay* me? Because I'd pay people to let me do it!"

"What about makeup artist?" I reminded her. "I thought that was going to be your career."

Margaret looked torn for a moment, but then

she brightened. "I know. I'll organize the wedding, *and* I'll do the bride's makeup. I'll call it the Full-Service Treatment."

Then she sank her head to her arms. "And that's another thing," she groaned. "My mother says the only makeup she's going to wear on Saturday is some lipstick, and she wants to put that on by herself. I don't know why she is even bothering to get married. There's only one reason in the world to get married, and that's to have a great wedding, the kind that's really fancy. This isn't going to be a real wedding at all."

"A real wedding is whatever the two people getting married want it to be," my mom said. "And your mother and Alan want it to be simple. I think simple weddings are the nicest."

This time I joined Margaret in the You-Must-Be-Kidding face—everyone knows that fancy is better than plain.

My mom hoisted herself out of her chair. She sponged off the table, then she eyed the high chair in the corner.

"Mom," I said, "it's clean. You wash it every day, plus you just painted it. It's covered with brand-new, never-been-dirtied paint."

My mother ignored me and started running hot water into a bucket.

Margaret tipped her head and watched my mother with a funny expression on her face, as if she'd never seen her before.

I leaned over and whispered into Margaret's ear. "She's gotten obsessed with cleaning and organizing stuff lately. It's called *nesting*. She'll be back to normal after the baby's born, but for now, she's a little crazy."

Margaret shot me a look that said she thought *I* was the crazy one here. She got up and stood right beside my mother, never mind the exploding belly, eyeing the high chair. "How about we boil it?" she suggested. "That would clean it *and* kill all the germs."

My mother looked at Margaret as if this was an incredible, brilliant, genius idea. Then she sighed. "I wish," she said. "But I don't have a big enough pot."

"No problem," Margaret said. "We'll take the tray off, and then unscrew the arms and the legs . . ."

I got out of there quick, in case whatever was wrong with them was catching.

Friday morning I slept as late as I wanted to. After breakfast, Zucchini and I made our parents a card. *HAPPY ANNIVERSARY!* it said. *WE SURE ARE GLAD YOU TWO MET!*

"If they hadn't," I explained to my brother, "we wouldn't be here. We'd be . . ."

Asparagus's jaw fell open. "Extinct? Like dinosaurs?"

"No, not like dinosaurs. We'd just be . . . not. Don't think about it, though, because it will make your head hurt."

Next, we built a fort out of the boxes the new air conditioners had come in. We made secret escape tunnels out of the leftover duct hose, and booby-trapped it with water balloons.

It was fun, but all the time I was waiting for it to be four o'clock, when my ashtray would be ready. The glazes we had painted on Wednesday night had looked like gray mud. But Astrid had promised that in the kiln, they would harden over the clay in bright colors, like melted jewels.

Finally the time came, and my mother and I drove over to her friend's pottery studio.

When Astrid opened the door, she smacked her cheeks and made pop-eyes at how big my mother's belly was. Then my mom admired Astrid's belly, which was about halfway pregnant. They side-hugged so their bellies wouldn't squash into each other.

We followed Astrid into her studio. "I've got to

cover some wet pots, then we'll
open the kiln," she said. She
handed me a lump of clay,
because artists know that
other artists like to make
something while they
are waiting, and then
she left. I started mold-
ing the clay into a toy
mouse for my kitten,
who's going to have a
birthday in the summer.

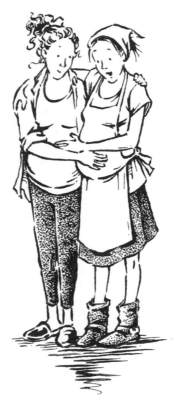

"Actually, I'm glad
we have this time alone
together," my mom said.
She patted the space on
the bench beside her.

This meant it was time for
a serious talk, so I sat down and

put on my I-Am-Seriously-Listening-to-You face,
which I invented early in my career. Here is how
you do it: find a place on your parent's face that is
right between the eyes. Stare there, and move in
close enough that you feel your own eyes starting
to cross just a little bit. Let your mouth hang open,

as though you are so fascinated by what your parent is saying, you are powerless to close it. This face always fools them.

"Clementine, I really hate it when you do that thing with your eyes— please stop. I want to talk to you about this feud you're having with your father."

"The sad-animal drawings?"

"No, not those. I like that you're doing those, in fact. You're presenting your side of something you care about. That's what artists do: when they care about something, they make art about it. And sometimes their art makes other people care too, although sometimes it doesn't. The problem is the other thing: your not speaking to him. Clementine, I'm sorry, but you can't force other people to believe something, no matter how much you believe it. And when you're having a disagreement with someone, it's always better to talk than not to. You need to start talking to your dad."

I dropped my head. My clay suddenly looked like a teardrop. I squished it into a ball. "I want to. I miss him so much. But I don't think I can anymore—every time I see him, I think about that cow. I'm still so mad, and it's as if the mad is blocking my throat. It feels like a big, sour lemon is stuck in there." As I said it, I felt my throat close down, as if the lemon was a dangerous one, one that could make me cry.

"I get that. But it happens: people you love are going to do things you hate sometimes. You can't stop talking to them, though. I'll leave it up to you to find the right thing to say to your father, and the right time to say it."

Just then Astrid came in. She walked over to

the kiln and checked the temperature gauge.

I stood and gave my mom a tug up. "Thanks," she said. "Now let's go see our pottery."

When Astrid opened the kiln, I have to admit I was a little disappointed. I guess I was expecting it to be like an oven where there's something delicious baking. It didn't smell like cookies or lasagna—in fact, I couldn't smell anything at all. And at first, I couldn't see anything either.

But then Astrid stuck a paddle into the kiln and pulled out a tray full of my mom's stars, which she had made for a new baby mobile. And my heart almost burst from the beauty.

Astrid was right about the glazes: the colors gleamed like jewels!

I held my breath as Astrid slid the paddle back into the kiln. I had used all the same glazes on my ashtray, but I had swirled them together. What if that made them turn back into mud? But when

she pulled it out, there on her paddle was the most
wonderful thing I had ever made. The blue and
the yellow glazes met in lime green smears spot-
ted with caramel and turquoise. Feathery purple
patches glittered with lemon sparks, and tangerine

curlicues crept through clouds of rose and gold.

My mom and I thanked Astrid about a hundred times for letting us use her kiln. Then we tucked Bubble Wrap around our pottery, packed everything into boxes, and carried them out to our car.

On the way home I kept staring into the open box beside me, where my ashtray sat.

"You look a little sad," my mom said, glancing back in the rearview mirror. "Is it going to be hard to give it away?"

"No," I said. "Well, a little. But it will be at Margaret's, so I can visit it. That's not it."

"So . . ."

I sighed. "Don't you wish we had all that stuff at home?" I asked. "A studio like Astrid has, with a kiln? We could make pottery every day. And other art, too—like stained glass, or papier-mâché, or wood carving—whenever we wanted!"

"I'd have a drawing table ten feet long," Mom said.

"And big easels for painting at. And a place to do mosaics," I said. "I've always wanted to do mosaics!"

"And a forge for metal works, and a weaving loom, and a jewelry workshop," my mom added. She was practically drooling.

Once we got going with this dream, it was a little hard to stop. "How about a place to get a massage for when your back hurts from bending over your drawing table?" my mom suggested.

"And someone baking chocolate chip cookies—I could always use chocolate chip cookies when I'm making art," I said.

Mom laughed. "Well, I'd settle for a good coffee shop next door." She glanced back in the mirror again, and her face was serious. "You know, Clementine, you could have a studio of your own.

There's plenty of room in the basement. Your dad could set you up with a nice space—you should ask him."

"Maybe," I said. Although even then I knew I couldn't. If you're really mad at someone, you don't get to ask him for a favor. No, if I had to talk to my father, my first words were definitely not going to be *Will you make me an art studio?*

CHAPTER
8

Saturday morning at breakfast, Radish and I gave our parents their card, which they loved. Then I brought up the problem of our no-name baby again. "Have you decided anything yet?" I asked, being careful to point my words at my mother.

"We're talking about a few possibilities," she answered. "Nothing definite."

"Remember, it should be a thing-name," I said.

"Well, I still like Noodle," my dad said. He got

up and scraped his plate into the sink. "It's a thing, it's a food, and what kid wouldn't love to be called Noodle?"

My brother sprayed English muffin into his apple juice, he laughed so hard at this. But my mom ignored my dad and so did I, although okay, fine—I thought he was pretty funny.

Just then my father's beeper went off. "The building inspector's here to check out the new air conditioners," he said. "I won't be long." As he was putting the beeper back on his belt, he stopped, frozen, staring at it. His face lit up. "That's it! The perfect thing-name!" he cried. "Beeper!"

Corn sprayed the rest of his English muffin into his juice at that. Then he slid out of his chair and wrapped his arms around my mom, laughing "Beeper! Beeper! Beeper!" into her belly.

My mother rolled her eyes and waved my dad

away, but she was laughing
now too. I turned my head
so nobody would see how
much I wanted to join in the
beeper-fun, or how lonely
I must look because I
couldn't.

"Of course it's a
shame," my dad said,
buckling on his tool belt,
"to give up a great name
like Noodle." Then his
face lit up again. "So
we'll hyphenate it:
Noodle-Beeper. There,
I'm glad that's settled."
As the door shut behind
him, we could still hear

his voice in the hallway. "Or maybe Beeper-Noodle. Oh, yeah, that's even better. . . ."

I let myself laugh a little bit as I cleared my plate off the table. When I went back to get my mom's plate, I noticed something strange: she didn't have one. "How come you didn't eat breakfast?" I asked. "Are you okay?"

"I'm okay," my mom answered. "Just not hungry."

"Well, what about Beeper-Noodle?"

She patted her tummy. "The baby doesn't seem hungry either. How about we put that mobile together now?"

And for the rest of the morning, we strung the pottery stars with invisible fishing line, and then hung them from some driftwood branches we had collected at the beach last summer. Well, my mother and I did—my brother just stomped on the Bubble Wrap the stars had been wrapped in.

It took a long time, because the stars were all different—different colors, different shapes, different sizes—and we had to figure out the perfect spots for them all. They had to balance each other, and be hung where each one looked its best. They also had to be far enough apart that when a breeze moved them they wouldn't clack into each other and get hurt. When it was finished, we hung it in the window near where the crib was waiting.

Okra had gotten pretty tired out from all that dinosaur stomping, so my mother thought it was a good time to wrestle him into a bath. I stayed in my parents' bedroom, looking into the empty crib and trying to imagine it filled with a brother or a sister. "When are you coming?" I whispered. "Are you going to be a dud? Are you going to be half rat? And what's your name going to be, for real?"

Then I went back into the living room and took my ashtray out to admire it for the last few minutes before I had to give it away. It was even more beautiful than before, and I decided right then that I was going to make another one, one that would live in *our* house. The problem was, nobody in my family smoked.

Just as I was trying to figure out what else could live in an ashtray besides a pipe, my dad came in. "Boy, I wish I had something like this to store my beeper in," he sighed. He took it off his belt and tapped it down the slide to the swimming pool, then set it down on the bed. "This would be perfect, all right," he said.

I looked up and gave him a smile. But my throat hurt just from looking at him, and my eyes were getting a little watery. *Remember the cow in the meat loaf,* I told myself. Then I picked up the wedding present ashtray and headed for the door.

"Time to give it away, Sport?" my father asked.

I nodded—nodding isn't speaking—and walked out to the elevator.

"Don't be long," he called after me. "I need to talk to you about tonight. Your mother's pretty tired, with the baby coming soon, so for dinner—"

Luckily the elevator doors opened then, and I hurried inside. If the rest of his sentence involved Mrs. Jacobi and a meat loaf, I didn't want to hear it. I pressed the button for Margaret's floor.

Because I knew Margaret would be dressed up in her new outfit and shoes by now, I practiced smacking my forehead and saying, "WOW!" on the way up to the room.

It was Mitchell who opened the door, though, and I almost dropped the ashtray. He wore a suit and tie, and his hair was combed into perfect lines. He looked like a movie star, except one that was still thirteen.

He said, "Hi," but I couldn't say *Hi* back. I could only stare at him.

"I know," he said. "I wanted to wear my baseball uniform, but Margaret insisted on this. Does it look dumb?"

And I still couldn't speak. I felt really strange. I felt . . . at first, I couldn't even think of a word to describe it.

And then I did: *glozzled*.

Which could N-O-T, *not* be right, because I did N-O-T, *not* love Mitchell.

Just then, luckily, I figured it out. When Mitchell says the word *baseball*, you can practically see the

love stars beaming from his chest. Because I was standing right in front of him, I must have gotten hit with some of them.

"Um, could you stand sideways, please?" I asked him, glad that my voice sounded only a little glozzled. "And don't say *baseball* again, okay?"

Mitchell gave me a funny look, but he turned sideways, and then I ran past him down the hall.

When I opened the door to Margaret's room, I saw her standing in front of her mirror. She looked like a big, pink girl-cake—a really fancy one, with frosting flowers and ribbons and bows trailing off her. I put the ashtray down so I could smack my head with both hands and say, "WOW!" And I wasn't even pretending.

Margaret spun around then, which was kind of a mistake in those shoes. Her ankles collapsed, and Margaret looked stunned to find them on the floor so suddenly. She snapped her ankles back up

again and took a few steps toward me.

"Wow," I said again, and okay, fine—this time I was pretending a little bit. "Not too wobbly!"

Just then Margaret's mother came in. She must have been beaming love stars, like Mitchell, because looking at her also made me feel a little glozzled.

"You look really nice," I told her. It wasn't just

that she was wearing a pretty yellow suit and a hat. It was more that her face had an I-Must-Be-Dreaming look I had never seen on it before.

Margaret looked a little glozzled now too, as if she'd been clonked by her mother's beaming love stars. She hobbled over and gave her mother a hug. "She let me put some blush on her," Margaret explained to me. "Coral Shimmer. That's why she looks so great."

Margaret's mother said it was time to go to the courthouse, and then she left to call for a taxi. I said, "Happy wedding!" and I got up to leave too.

"Here's the ashtray," I said, handing it over to Margaret. "All baked clean."

And this time it was Margaret saying, "Wow!" She took it right into her hands without making me wash it in the sink, so I knew she really liked it. "Thanks," she said. "See you this afternoon."

"What do you mean?" I asked. "I thought you

were going to the hotel after the wedding."

"I am," Margaret said, looking surprised.
"You're going too. Your father called my father

a little while ago to ask if you could stay over tonight. He said he was going to tell you about it."

"Oh," I said. "Right."

Although, suddenly, everything felt the opposite of right.

CHAPTER

9

Back in my apartment, my dad was just coming out of my parents' bedroom.

"She's resting, Sport," he said as he closed the door. "I'm taking her out to dinner tonight to celebrate our anniversary—give her a treat. You kids are going to have a treat too. Your brother's sleeping over with Uncle Frank and Aunt Claire, and you're going to spend the night with Margaret in the fanciest hotel in Boston. Go pack a bag. Toothbrush and pajamas."

I ran into my room and stuffed my pajamas and

toothbrush into my backpack. Then I added the rolled-up poster of my old cat Polka Dottie that I sometimes—okay, fine: almost always—need to look at before I go to sleep.

I patted Moisturizer good-bye, then I walked down the hall. At my parents' door, I knocked at exactly the right loudness: quiet enough that if my mom was asleep it wouldn't wake her, but loud enough that if she was awake she could hear it. My mom said to come on in.

"You look like a volcano," I told her as I climbed carefully onto the bed beside her.

"I know," she said. She put her book down. "So you're going to a fancy hotel tonight, I hear. Very la-di-da."

"Yep. How come you're in bed?"

"Resting. Being a volcano takes a lot of energy. I have to save up for the big eruption."

Then I thought of something I'd never thought

of before. "Will it hurt?" I asked. "The big eruption?"

My mom shrugged. "Mostly, it's going to be a lot of work. So I really need to get some extra rest, especially if I'm going out tonight. You go on now, and have fun, okay?"

I said okay, then I kissed her good-bye. A few minutes later, my brother and I got into the car with my dad and drove to Uncle Frank and Aunt Claire's.

"Tuna fish or egg salad?" Aunt Claire asked, holding out a platter of sandwiches.

Cauliflower and I picked egg salad, but my dad took tuna. "Fish have feelings, too, you know," I muttered into my sandwich, but my dad had gone off to eat with Uncle Frank on the deck.

After lunch, I reminded Aunt Claire and Uncle

Frank that my brother is allergic to peanuts, which they know, but I felt better saying it. And then my dad and I drove to the Park Plaza Hotel.

On the way, my dad talked to me about some things we could do on our summer vacation—try all thirty-seven flavors at the ice cream shop, camp out on the top of our building to watch for shooting stars, collect enough pigeon feathers to make a pair of wings. They sounded great, but I made myself remember the tuna fish in his sandwich and the cow in the meat loaf and didn't answer him. And then, after we parked and were walking up to the hotel, he stopped to crouch down and look me straight in the eyes.

"Not talking to each other doesn't work—not in this family," he said. "I appreciate that you feel strongly about not eating animals, but I don't feel the same way. So how about a compromise? In our home, vegetarian is the rule. For the rest of the year, I'm willing to try that. But out of the house, when I'm visiting Uncle Frank, or we're at a restaurant, I'll choose what I want. That's the best I can do, and you're going to have to accept that. All right?"

I shrugged and scooped my head around in a circle: not yes, but not no, either.

"Well, at least promise me you'll think about it."

For a minute, I did think about his compromise. Good: mostly my father wouldn't eat animals. Bad: sometimes he still would. I felt like half of the dangerous lemon instantly disappeared from my throat. But here is the news about lemons: even with only half of one in your throat, it's still hard to talk. So I just nodded about the "think about it" promise, and didn't say a word.

My dad stood up and then we walked up the hotel driveway together. A tall man in a uniform greeted us. "Welcome to the Boston Park Plaza,"

he said with a bow. Then he held the door open and swooped his arm like a game show host to guide us in. "Will you be staying with us this evening?"

I bowed back as my dad answered, "My daughter will be checking in."

The doorman smiled as if this was the news he had been waiting for all his life. He bowed again and asked if he could take my luggage.

"My luggage?" I asked with another bow.

He tipped his eyebrows to my backpack.

"Oh, my *luggage*," I said. I wriggled my backpack off and took out the poster of Polka Dottie. "I'd better carry this myself," I told him as I handed the backpack to him.

It was a good thing he'd taken my backpack, because when I saw the inside of that lobby, I almost fell right over. A huge, glittering chandelier hung from the golden ceiling, which looked a hundred feet high. The floors were marble, and there were shiny leather couches and satin drapes everywhere you looked. I gave my dad's hand a squeeze in case the fanciness of this lobby was making him feel bad about our plain lobby at home, and he squeezed mine back.

At the registration desk, the doorman handed my backpack to another man in a uniform. "This is Raoul, who will be your bellhop," he said. "He will assist you to your room."

The lady behind the desk wore a name tag that said LINDSEY. We gave her Margaret's father's name and waited while she checked a list. I figured it was probably CRIMINALS WHO AREN'T ALLOWED INTO THE PARK PLAZA HOTEL. "You don't have to worry, I've never been in jail," I told her. "But if a kid named Baxter ever tries to get in, watch out."

Lindsey said that was good to know, and then she handed me a tiny envelope with a plastic card inside and pointed us to the elevators.

The elevator doors gleamed like golden mirrors. My dad must have seen me wondering if the condo association in our building would go for bronze elevator doors, because he shook his head sadly and said, "Not a chance."

Raoul followed us into the elevator. He tried to press the buttons, but I told him he could take

a few minutes off, because I am an expert in operating elevators. On the way up, Raoul's eyes kept glancing at my poster, so I unrolled it and let him look at Polka Dottie.

"That is quite a cat," he said, after he'd admired her for a few floors.

"She *was*," I said, rolling her back up safely. "She died last spring, and I'm still sad about that. But in the fall I got a new kitten, who's having a birthday in the summer and then he won't be a kitten anymore, he'll be a cat. Like Polka Dottie was, except he's different from her, which I'm glad about. My birthday's in September . . . I'll be nine. And we're having a baby soon. Do you have a tattoo?"

But before Raoul could answer my question, we were at the sixteenth floor. I told my feet not to run down the long hallway, and for once they listened to me, although they weren't very happy about it.

At the room, Raoul showed me how to slide the card down the slot in the door handle, and then a green light flashed and the lock clicked open.

Margaret's father welcomed us in and started talking with my father, while Raoul put my backpack on a luggage stand. Behind him, I saw Margaret sitting on a couch with her foot propped up on pillows. Her ankle was wrapped up like a mummy, and there was a pair of crutches beside her. "Margaret," I gasped, "what happened?"

From the way Margaret's lips were pressed together, I could tell she didn't want to tell me what happened. Which told me what happened: she fell off her shoes.

"A fashion accident," she said at last. Then she lowered her head to glare over at her brother. She sharpened her voice and shot him a word-arrow: "It was *worth it*."

My dad secret-handed me a folded-up dollar

bill and then nodded toward Raoul. "Tip," he whispered.

So I secret-handed Raoul the dollar bill and whispered, "Tip." I also told him that nobody had ever carried my backpack better than he had—except me, of course—and this made him even happier than the dollar bill did. He bent down and tugged his collar aside to show me a tattoo of a dragon winding around his neck, and then he left.

When I went over to ask Margaret about her foot, her chin started to tremble. She picked up Mascara and hugged him tight. Then she ordered me into the bathroom so I could admire the *Sanitized for Your Protection!* tape wrapped around the glasses. I figured it was really so she could wipe any tears off her face—Margaret doesn't like people to see her when she's crying—so I stayed in there a little while. And the bathroom was great all right: marble everything, and Margaret had been telling the truth about the individually wrapped soaps. There were other single-serving-size things too—tiny bottles of shampoo and conditioner and moisturizer. The towels were folded into crisp fans, and the toilet paper ends were tucked into perfect triangles.

All the while I was in there, I kept an ear out

for my dad, who was still chatting with Margaret's dad.

"Well, thanks again for having her," I heard him say. "We really appreciate it. We'll give you a call tomorrow." Then he called out, "Bye, Clementine," and I heard him leave.

And suddenly, I didn't want to be alone in that fancy bathroom anymore.

CHAPTER

10

Margaret insisted on giving me a tour of the hotel suite from the couch. She read from a la-di-blah-blah hotel booklet and used her crutch to point out the *many elegant guest features for your enjoyment.*

While she read, I unpacked my things. I put my pajamas in the bureau, my toothbrush in the bathroom, and my poster beside the bed. And there at the bottom of my backpack was a surprise: my report card. I had forgotten to give it to my parents Thursday night.

I opened it. It was the usual stuff: all A's in

math, all not-A's in everything else. But at the bottom was a note from my teacher—the good-bye words he'd been trying to say to me all week. I read it, then crumpled it up and stuffed it into my back pocket.

"Why don't you kids go explore the hotel lobby?" Margaret's dad suggested. "I've got some work to do." He picked up his phone and sat down at the desk.

Margaret made it out to the hall on her crutches, but you could tell it was pretty hard work. Mitchell and I looked at each other, then we looked at the room service cart across the way, then we looked at Margaret.

"Oh, no," she said. "I'm not getting on there with all those dirty dishes. That thing is crawling with germs."

But Mitchell and I explained that she could curl up on the bottom shelf, which was empty, and she grumbled and said okay. "But put down a sterilized towel first."

We did, and then Margaret climbed on. Mitchell and I grabbed the handle, ready to roll. Before we even took one step, though, a bellhop turned the corner in front of us. It was Raoul. He was wearing a frown, but you could tell he was having a hard time keeping it in place. "Allow me to take that off your hands," he said.

Mitchell and I helped Margaret off the cart and back onto her crutches.

Margaret hopped over to the door and slid the key-card through the slot. "You two go. I need to rehearse for my commercial," she said, flapping her hands at us.

"There's nothing to rehearse, Margaret," I heard her dad call out. "You won't have any lines. You just have to look happy if you get to go to the water park and sad if you don't."

But Margaret insisted, so Mitchell and I took off. He showed me the vending machine and the ice machine, and a brass-plated mail slot where you could mail a letter right into the wall. Then we took the elevator down to the lobby. And that's where I saw the best thing of all: two thrones. I am not even kidding about that. Big green leather thrones, set up high on a platform.

"Wow," I said. "So kings and queens come here, too?"

"Nah, Dude-ette," Mitchell said. "It's a shoe-shine station. Up you go."

I climbed up onto the throne and Mitchell pretended to shine my sneakers, and then I pretended to pay him, and then he pretended I didn't give him a big-enough tip. Then he climbed up on the throne, and I pretended his sneakers were too smelly for me to work on, and that was the end of that game, so we jumped down.

"How was the wedding?" I asked, as we wandered down the halls, poking our heads into all the rooms that weren't locked.

"Oh, fine," Mitchell answered. "At least until Margaret fell."

"Did she ruin the ceremony?"

"No, they were done with the *I do* part. Margaret was supposed to walk over and sprinkle them with rose petals at the end. But she insisted on skipping, and boom! Sister down. I had to wear that suit for an extra hour while we waited in the emergency room. But it's over now. And hey, it's summer! No school! Ball games every day!"

I gave Mitchell a *Yay! Everything's GREAT!* grin, but I guess he could tell it was fake.

"What's wrong?" he asked. "Aren't you happy it's summer?"

"Oh, I am," I said. "My grandparents are going to come when the baby's born, and I'll get to sleep on the couch for a whole week. My uncle's going to teach me some magic tricks, and I'm going to build a boat with a glass floor, and learn to ride a unicycle. Plus, I'm happy about no school. I just wish I had said good-bye to my teacher."

"You didn't do it? How come?"

"Well . . ." I started to tell Mitchell that I hated saying good-bye, but now I knew that wasn't it. So I told him the real reason. "Because he kept saying how I was ready for fourth grade, and it isn't true. I haven't done all the stuff he said—all the growing and changing things. He's wrong."

"Like what?"

"Like . . ." I pulled my report card out and read from it. "'Clementine, you've made such great progress in controlling your impulses, and thinking ahead about consequences.' That stuff. I hate when people say good things about me if they're wrong."

Mitchell skidded to a stop so hard, I almost expected to see sparks flaming out of his heels. "Dude-ette, are you *kidding*?" he cried. "Margaret says you've gone a whole week without speaking to your father—is that true?"

I looked up at the fancy clock in the lobby. "Well, almost. In an hour and seven minutes it will be a full week. So what?"

"And you haven't slipped up once?"

I shook my head. "I almost did, lots of times. I wanted to talk to him, but then I'd remember just in time that speaking to him would be not not-speaking to him."

Mitchell pulled his baseball from his pocket, smiling. "So, let's see," he said, tossing the ball up and catching it. "You *controlled your impulses* to talk to your dad, because *you thought ahead about the consequences*. For a *whole week*." He caught the ball and handed it to me. "It kills me to say this, Dude-ette, but your teacher's right."

Oh.

My teacher was right.

I *had* changed this year.

Which meant I could have said good-bye to him.

But now it was too late.

When we got back, Margaret's father handed us the room service menus. We chose our meals—a grilled cheese and pickle sandwich and a strawberry parfait for me—and then I got to call on the phone and order everything. Half an hour later, two waiters brought a cart into the room and started sweeping silver lids off plates, just like on the cooking shows I watch with my mom.

As we ate, we played a game Margaret invented called Fancy Folks. How you play it is this: hold your fork with your pinkie finger sticking out, squeeze your mouth into a tight *O*, and take a teeny, tiny nibble. Put your fork down after every bite and tap your napkin to your lips three times and say, "Oh, my, isn't this *too* scrumptious!"

That's the whole boring game, and I am not even kidding about this.

At seven o'clock, Mitchell and his dad went into their room to watch the Red Sox on their television. Margaret and I went into her bedroom, and she picked up the remote. "My dad says we can watch a movie." She clicked the TV on and started scrolling down the list.

"You pick, Margaret," I decided. "Just not *Beauty and the Beast.*"

"Why not?" Margaret asked. "I thought you loved that movie, especially the dancing part."

"I do," I said. "I did. I don't want to think about the dancing part tonight, that's all."

But it was too late for that. Margaret picked a movie about some princesses who formed a rock band, and we watched it twice—once on the floor and once in our beds, and then we fell asleep. But in the middle of the night, Mascara jumped up onto my bed and woke me up. And there, in my head, was the dancing part of *Beauty and the Beast.*

So I thought, Okay, fine—I give up. I *will* think about the *Beauty and the Beast* time.

When I was little, my father took me to see the movie. There was nobody else in the theater, because it had been playing so long everybody on the whole planet had already seen it. I had already seen it, too—six times. But I wanted to watch it again, because I loved the part where Belle and the Beast dance while the teapot sings. Since there was no one there to yell at us, when that part came, my father took me up onto the stage in front of the screen, and we danced. My father and I danced right there with Belle and the Beast.

On the way home, I thanked him and thanked him.

My dad laughed. "Let's hope you remember this when you're really mad at me about something."

"I'm never going to be mad at you," I promised, surprised that he could even think up such a bad thing.

My dad had pulled the car off the road and parked. "Yes, you will," he said. "Look, you've got me for a father, and I've got you for a daughter, for a long, long time. It's a life sentence. And since we're two different people—which is good, by the way—we're going to have lots of disagreements. We're going to get really angry with each other sometimes."

"No, we won't, Dad! I'll always remember you let me dance with Belle and the Beast, and I'll never, ever, be mad at you."

"That's not how it works in families, Sport," he'd said. "I'm going to want you to be you, and you're going to want me to be me. But that will mean arguments, and sometimes they might be awful. But how about this: when we're really, really furious with each other, we'll remember dancing with the movie, and we'll figure a way around whatever we're mad about. Deal?"

I had shaken hands with him, and we'd gotten back on the road. As we drove home that after-

noon, I'd decided that he was just wrong—we weren't going to argue about stuff and get angry at each other.

This week, though, I found out he'd been right: we *were* different people, and it sure did make me mad at him. And now, as I sat in that fancy hotel room with Mascara's purring making me miss my own kitten, and with the midnight noises of hotel strangers making me miss my own family, I was really hoping he was right about the last part, too.

As soon as I woke up the next morning, I asked if I could call home. I had decided during the night that I was ready to try saying one word to my father. *Hi* was a nice short one to start with.

"Let's wait," Margaret's father said. "Your father said he'd call when they were ready."

So we ordered room service breakfast, and like before, two waiters brought it up and made a big production about uncovering everything, even though it was just regular blueberry pancakes.

This time we ate playing a game Mitchell

invented, Raised by Wolves, which I probably shouldn't tell how to play. It was a lot more fun that Fancy Folks, that's all I'm going to say about that.

After breakfast, Margaret positioned herself in front of the television to rehearse her commercial. "Just pretend you're seeing me inside the screen, not in front of it. With makeup on. And without the crutches."

Margaret stretched her face around for a while, and then she asked me what I thought.

"Great!" I said. "You looked really sad you couldn't go to the water park!"

"You're not paying attention," Margaret grumbled. "I was being one of the lucky kids who *does* get to go."

But I was paying attention: I was paying attention to the phone that kept on not ringing. Which—okay, fine—wasn't really fair to Margaret.

"Try again," I said. "I'll really watch this time."

Margaret made a lot more faces, then she asked me what I thought again.

"I don't know, Margaret," I said. "You still looked kind of . . . horrified, actually."

"Well," Margaret admitted, "that was part of it, I guess. I was imagining being really happy to go to that water park, then I started imagining all the germs that must be swimming around in that water. . . ." Margaret rolled her eyes and shuddered hard.

And then I thought of something Margaret was N-O-T, *not* going to like. "Um, where are they going to film this commercial?" I asked carefully.

"Oh, at my father's studio, I guess," Margaret answered. "Or, wait . . . maybe . . . no, not at the . . ." She turned white. "Dad!" she yelled into the other room, "I changed my mind. I want to play one of the kids who *doesn't* have to go to the water park!"

Just then, there was a knock on the door. When Margaret's dad came out and opened it, there stood two cleaning ladies. Between them were a serious-looking vacuum and a big cart loaded with

linens and cleaning supplies. Margaret crutched across the room so fast she nearly toppled over. When she leaned over to see what was on the cart, she looked like a cartoon pirate opening a treasure chest.

Mitchell and his dad left to go get the Sunday paper, but I stayed behind to watch Margaret watch the cleaning ladies. Also—okay, fine—I stayed behind in case the phone rang. Which it didn't.

Margaret followed the cleaning ladies around, asking questions and jotting their answers down in a notebook, which was a hard trick, since she was balancing on crutches. Every time she asked if she could help them, they looked at each other and shook their heads No. But finally, when they were almost finished, Margaret begged to vacuum the last bit of carpet, by the door, and they said, Okay, if it means that much to you. I propped her up so she could balance on one foot, and she vacuumed piles of imaginary dirt from that floor.

This put Margaret in such a good mood that when Mitchell came back she let us play with her crutches. This time, I invented the game. How you play What Happened to Your Foot? is this: One person is on crutches, and the others pop into the room and gasp, "What happened to your foot?" Then the crutch person has to come up with a new story every time, really fast.

Margaret quit after just a few turns, saying, "Oh, who cares how it happened?" and hopped over to flop onto the couch. But Mitchell and I kept it up for a really long time.

"I don't know! I woke up and it was missing!"

"Parachute didn't open!"

"Trapeze broke!"

"Cannibal socks!"

"Bone-melting aliens!"

"Runaway steamroller!"

"Alligators in my bathtub!"

"Elephant stampede!"

"Toe sharks!"

"Heel bees!"

"Heel bees?"

"Heel bees!"

I finally won when Mitchell tried, "Flying catch, World Series!" for a second time.

This game made us all hungry for lunch, so we ordered room service again, and this time we didn't play any game at all, we just ate. After that, Margaret and I watched the rock band princesses movie again, and then finally, finally, the phone rang.

Margaret's father answered it, and he winked  over at me to let me know it was my family. I figured my parents must have had a really great date, because he smiled while he listened, and then he said, "Great,"

"Wonderful," and "Congratulations," lots of times.

"No, I won't," he said next, still smiling. "Not a word." Then he hung up. "Time to go home, Clementine," he said to me.

I stuffed my things into my backpack and hurried over to the door.

"I always take the little bottles from the bathroom when I leave," Margaret said. "You can take them this time."

I went into the bathroom and brought them all out. "The shampoo will be for my mom, and the conditioner is for my dad. I'll give the bar of soap to my brother, to give him the hint he should get clean once in a while. The bottle of moisturizer is for my kitten, since that's his name." I dropped them all into my backpack and thanked Margaret for being so nice.

"What about something for yourself?" Margaret's father asked. "Something to remember your stay?"

"There's nothing else in the bathroom," I said.

Margaret's father beckoned me to follow him over to the desk. He pointed.

And there was the best thing of all: a sheet of creamy writing paper and an envelope that both said *The Boston Park Plaza* in fancy lettering.

"Really?" I asked. "I could have that?"

"That's what it's there for. The Park Plaza would be delighted."

CHAPTER

12

At my building, I said "Good-bye, thank you!" to Margaret's dad as fast as I could and ran down to my apartment. When I opened the door, something felt different, but I couldn't tell what it was at first. My kitten was asleep on the windowsill, my dad was conked out on the couch, and my mom was curled up against him. She put a *shhh!*-finger to her lips, then she looked down and smiled. On her lap was a loaf of bread, tightly wrapped up in a soft yellow blanket.

I looked again.

The loaf of bread had a little squished-up face.

"Oh!" I whispered. Very carefully, I climbed up on the couch beside my mom.

"Say hello to your sister," she said.

I said hello and bent closer to get a better look. And let me tell you, there was not much to see.

The good news was: at least my new sister wasn't half rat. She had ten tiny fingers, and at the tips were ten even tinier fingernails, not claws. No fur, no whiskers, and no sign of a tail coming out of the blanket.

But I have to say, the bad news about my new sister was pretty bad. Her face was red and lumpy—two lumps sticking out on the sides were probably ears, and I hoped the one in the middle was a nose. She was mostly bald, with just a few little tufts of hair that looked like cotton candy. If you let the air out of a teeny-tiny, wrinkled-up old-man balloon, you'd have a good idea of what my new sister looked like. Not so hot. Here is a picture of that:

Before I could tell my mother how sorry I was that her second daughter was so homely, Aunt Claire and Uncle Frank came in with my brother. Spinach took one look at the baby, then ran into his room, howling. My dad woke up and went after him.

My aunt and uncle pulled up chairs in front of the couch. My mom unwrapped the baby so they could see her.

I patted my mom's shoulder—it must be pretty sad to have to show this baby girl after having one like me.

"Oh, my goodness," Aunt Claire exclaimed. "She looks just like Clementine did!"

"Exactly the same!" Uncle Frank agreed. "Same hair, same nose, same everything! Beautiful, absolutely beautiful!"

I looked at my sister again. And a miracle must have happened, because now Uncle Frank was right . . . she was absolutely beautiful!

"What's her name?" my aunt asked.

My mom shook her head. "She came a little early—caught us by surprise. We'd better pick one soon."

The baby woke up then and decided she was hungry. My mom started to feed her, and Uncle Frank and Aunt Claire put a casserole in the refrigerator and left.

My dad came out with Garbanzo Bean and plunked him down with his dinosaur book. Then he turned to me. "Clementine," he said, "we've had a call from the Pentagon. It's time for the Final Debriefing."

The Pentagon is a secret project my dad and I have been working on since we found out about the new baby. It's a table with five sides—one for everybody in our new five-person family—and my dad and I built it together, every single board and nail of it. *The Final Debriefing* was the code we'd decided to use when it was time for us to show the present to my mom.

My mom just gave us the puzzled look she always gives us when we talk about the Pentagon, then she went back to feeding our baby.

My dad closed the kitchen door, and being absolutely silent, we carried our old four-sided kitchen table out into the hall. Then I followed him into the work-shop. We tied a big purple bow around the new table, and very quietly carried it into the kitchen and set the chairs around it.

"You stay here," my dad whispered. "I'll go get the troops."

When my mother came into the kitchen, her mouth fell into a giant *O*. It was a good thing my dad had taken the baby, because she would have dropped her for sure, she was so surprised.

My father pulled out a chair and helped my mother sit down. Then he put our baby into her lap, and he and I took turns explaining the whole story of how we made the Pentagon.

My brother fell asleep at the table from being so bored about hearing about our carpentry stuff, but my mom just kept getting more and more excited. "Five sides . . . one for everybody . . . made it yourselves . . . such beautiful wood . . . kept it a secret . . ."

Usually when my mother can't finish her sentences it's because she's too mad. But this time

her face wore the I-Must-Be-Dreaming expression.

She held our baby close. "What a family, we are," she said. "What a family."

Then she leaned over and told me to hold out my arms.

I did, and into them, she placed our little baby.

"Brand-new," Mom said. "Just born at 12:01 this morning."

My sister was warm, and smelled sweet, like sugar and grass. Her head nestled like a grapefruit in the crook of my elbow, between Sirius and Vega. It looked as if the freckle-stars were protecting her, but they didn't need to, because I was strong and careful. I was never going to let anything happen to her.

I looked around at everyone then—my not-so-little brother conked out in a puddle of drool on our new table; my mother looking at me proudly, because she knew I wouldn't drop our baby; and my father, who ate Mrs. Jacobi's meat loaf, but who also built this table with me.

Then I looked down at my sister, born on the

summer solstice, who was just a few hours old. She didn't even know yet what a great family she'd gotten born into, or who she was going to be in the world. But she was peeking from her blanket as if she was ready to get started on finding out.

And two things happened at the same time! I figured out the perfect name for my new sister. And I knew who I wanted to say it to first.

"Mom," I said, "would you please tell Dad that I have something to whisper in his ear?"

My mother smiled at my father. My father smiled at my mother. Then they both grinned at me as though I was the winning ticket in the kid lottery. My dad came over and gave me a kiss on the top of my head, then crouched down beside me.

I whispered our baby's name in his ear.

"Perfect," he said. "That is absolutely perfect."

He told the name to my mom, and she said, "Perfect!" too.

And then I told it to my sister. "The sign in the lobby is for you," I said. "Today really is your first day. Welcome, Summer."

Dear Mr. D'matz,
Good-bye. I'm sorry I didn't say good-bye before. But before, I didn't know that I knew that speaking to someone would mean not not-speaking to him.
So you were right, I really learned a lot in third grade.
I'm not sure I'm going to do great in fourth grade, but I guess I'm ready to try.
Your ~~best hardest~~ favorite student,
Clementine

P.S. YET!
And she is ASTOUNDISHING!!!!!!!

The BOSTON
PARK PLAZA

50 PARK PLAZA AT ARLINGTON STREET   BOSTON, MA 0286 | TEL 7426 2000

IF YOU ENJOYED THE
CLEMENTINE BOOKS, LOOK FOR

Waylon!
One Awesome Thing

SARA PENNYPACKER

PICTURES BY
Marla Frazee

1
———

Waylon craned his neck. "Moon at the nearest point in its orbit—check. Clouds—check. But Joe, I'm telling you—"

"Are you sure about the clouds?" Beside him, Joe squinted at the sky. "They look so fluffy."

"Oh, they have plenty of mass," Waylon assured him. "A medium-sized cumulous cloud weighs as much as eighty elephants. But remember, the effect will barely be—"

"Don't forget the Airbus A380. That plane is huge. There it is, on the horizon." Joe flattened himself against the brick wall and chalked a mark at the top of his head.

Waylon sighed. Joe used to be the shortest kid in the class. He was pretty much normal-size now, thanks to a recent growth spurt, but he was still height-crazy. Last week Waylon had made the mistake of mentioning to him that Skylab astronauts had each grown two inches due to zero gravity. "That's it!" Joe had cried. "Gravity is what's keeping me down! You're science-y—do something!" He'd been pestering Waylon ever since.

"Remind me how this is going to work?" Joe asked now.

"Something really dense and really close, like the earth, has a lot of gravity," Waylon explained again. "But you could counteract it a little bit by stacking the moon, the clouds, and the Airbus above you. But seriously, it probably won't be enough to notice."

"How much?"

"Maybe an angstrom, which is really small, Joe! It takes about twenty-five million angstroms to make an inch."

"I'll take it!" Joe said. He pressed his shoulders to the wall and grinned.

Actually, Waylon was kind of excited, too. He was buying a special journal this weekend. In it, he would record his life's work as a scientist. Lately he'd been concentrating on gravity, and he was expecting a big breakthrough soon. If today's experiment worked, *Counteracted gravity to help a friend get taller* would look great on the first page of his new journal. "Here comes that plane, Joe," he cried. "Get ready!"

Just then, Arlo Brody ran up. He head-butted Waylon on the shoulder—not hard, but still, Waylon went sprawling.

Arlo jerked his thumb, and Joe trotted off with a grateful look on his face, as though he'd been waiting all recess for someone to send him away, never mind the getting-taller nonsense.

Arlo Brody was like that—he only had to suggest something, and a person magically felt that it would be an incredible honor to do that exact thing. Waylon suspected the phenomenon was related to Arlo's dreadlocks, which sprang out of his head like a crown. Arlo sure acted as if he was king of the whole school, and all the other kids acted like his subjects.

Waylon watched sadly as the clouds parted, and the Airbus zoomed away. It might be a long time before there was another perfect opportunity. But just then, Arlo smiled down at him, and Waylon felt as if he were basking in the warm glow of royal rays. His mouth automatically smiled back.

Arlo helped Waylon up. "I told you yesterday, you're on my team. You're supposed to spend recess with us. We have a name now. Shark-Punchers."

A bunch of boys had followed Arlo. They bared their shark teeth and head-butted each other.

"Shark-Punchers. That's our signature move," Arlo explained. "Get it?"

"Well, but . . . sharks can't punch." Waylon worried that might have sounded offensive, so he added a "Sorry."

Arlo threw a double punch at the air. "Sure they can. They have fins."

Waylon had no choice but to correct him. Science was science. "No. A shark's fins are hydrodynamic. They provide lift, like plane wings. And they pivot to change the angle of attack. Also, sharks use them to signal other sharks. But they can't punch."

"Whatever," Arlo said with a grin so big that Waylon's own cheeks hurt from returning it. "Look, it took me a while to decide whether to put you on my team or not. The blurting-out thing? Like the mucous stuff on Monday? Remember?"

Waylon remembered. Mrs. Fernman had just pointed to New Zealand on the map. Waylon had shot out of his seat. "There are these amazing glowworm caves there, except they're not really glowworms, they're fungus gnat maggots, and they drool long glow-in-thedark mucous strings to attract insects. It's so awesome!"

Everyone, except for Mrs. Fernman, had cracked up. This happened a lot when he shared something he'd learned on his favorite show, *Miracles of the Natural World*. He didn't understand the reaction—if someone had just told him something so interesting, he would be thanking that person, not laughing. But he had never minded it.

Until right now. *The "blurting-out thing"???*

"But even with the blurting-out thing," Arlo went on, "you're obviously a brain. I'm putting the brains and the jocks on my team."

Arlo beamed another shiny smile, and once more Waylon beamed it back.

Why had he done that? Waylon didn't want to be put on any team at all. He wished Arlo hadn't started the whole team thing in the first place. So why had his mouth just smiled back at Arlo?

Alien Hand Syndrome, he knew, was a rare disorder where a person loses control over one of his or her hands. It was his absolute favorite of all the conditions listed in Chapter Five, "Bizarre But True," in *The Science of Being Human*. But he'd never heard of Alien Mouth Syndrome.

Waylon forced his lips into a non-smiling position. "Are those the only choices?" he asked. "Brains or jocks?"

"You could be both, like me, but otherwise, yeah, one or the other. Except for Willy." Arlo crooked a finger at the Shark-Punchers, and Willy trotted out.

Willy looked anxious. Of course, he had

been looking anxious since Day One of fourth grade. This was because for the first time he wasn't in the same class as his twin sister, Lilly. For weeks now, he had been skittering around in a state of nervous panic.

"Willy's our artist," Arlo explained.

Waylon bit his lip to keep from saying *But Willy can only draw sharks. Clementine is the artist in our class*, because he knew what Arlo would say. Arlo had explained the rule yesterday: *Teams are boys only.*

"He's going to draw our logo. A shark, punching. Remember? All he has to learn to draw is the punching part. Easy. Right, Willy?"

Arlo seemed proud of this idea, but Willy looked petrified. Arlo threw an arm around his shoulders. "Forget the fins. Just make the shark's head a fist. With teeth. Okay?"

Willy looked around desperately. Waylon could tell he expected Lilly to be right beside him, telling him what to do.

"Disambiguation, Willy. Phantom Limb Syndrome," Waylon explained in a soothing tone. "When an arm or a leg gets amputated, people still feel like it's there. You have Phantom Sister Syndrome."

Now Willy appeared even more terrified of Waylon than he was of Arlo. "My sister wasn't *amputated!*" he howled. "She's just in *Room 4C!*" He dove back into the bunch of Shark-Punchers.

Arlo shot his pack a grinning thumbs-up, which they all returned. He spun back to Waylon. "We can get started now. Everyone's on a team."

Waylon scanned the playground. The girls

were sprinkled all around, playing or talking in little groups. But it was true that the fourth grade boys were divided. Half were clumped behind Arlo. The other half lined the fence, keeping a nervous eye on Arlo's clump. "What do we have to do?" Waylon asked.

"I told you yesterday. Stuff," Arlo answered. "Against the other team."

"Why?"

"Because they're against us."

"Why?"

"We're against them. Doing stuff. Come on, let's go. It's going to be cool."

Waylon considered the Shark-Punchers. Lots of his friends were there. Matt, whose mother worked at the aquarium. Matt let him explore behind the tanks with him whenever he wanted. Rasheed, who'd been building a duct-tape city with him since first grade. Zack, who was teaching him soccer.

Then he looked over at the other group. A lot of his friends were there, too. Charlie was the funniest kid in fourth grade. He and Waylon were working on a cartoon strip about astrophysics. Marco was studying to become a famous chef. He tried out new recipes on weekends and shared the leftovers with Waylon on Mondays. Next to Marco was Joe, who shared his dog, Buddy, with Waylon sometimes. Joe was so nice, he even let Waylon call Buddy Galaxy, and Buddy was so nice, he answered to it.

Waylon didn't get it. Until last week, everybody in the class had been friends, or at least they hadn't been not-friends. Why had Arlo gone and messed that up?

Just then, the Recess-Is-Over bell rang.

Arlo charged off to herd the Shark-Punchers to the front of the line. The other team gathered at the back.

Waylon stood alone in the middle. He felt a terrible collapsing sensation in his chest, as if a black hole had just swallowed his heart.

Collect all of the Clementines!

Praise for CLEMENTINE

★ "Fans of Judy Moody will welcome this portrait of another funny, independent third-grader."

—*Publishers Weekly* (starred review)

★ "Frazee's engaging pen-and-ink drawings capture the energy and fresh-faced expressions of the irrepressible heroine. . . . A delightful addition to any beginning chapter-book collection."

—*School Library Journal* (starred review)

Praise for
THE TALENTED CLEMENTINE

★ "Clementine is a true original. . . . Libraries will need multiple copies of this one, because early chapter-book readers will jump at the chance to spend another eventful week with Clementine."

—*School Library Journal* (starred review)

★ "Pennypacker once again demonstrates her keen insights into the third-grade mind with Clementine's priceless observations of the world around her."

—*Kirkus Reviews* (starred review)